Hollie & Figgs

The Missing Rainbow

Olive,
Let magic fill your life,
Happy Reading
Love from Hollie and Figgs ooo

Asharmanie '18

Hollie & Figgs

The Missing Rainbow

By Annette Sharman

Illustrations by Beth Hilliard

Matador
9 Priory Business Park,
Wistow Road, Kibworth Beauchamp,
Leicestershire. LE8 0RX
Tel: 0116 279 2299
Email: books@troubador.co.uk
Web: www.troubador.co.uk/matador
Twitter: @matadorbooks

ISBN 978 1788039 550

British Library Cataloguing in Publication Data.
A catalogue record for this book is available from the British Library.

Typeset in 20pt Chelsea Market by Troubador Publishing Ltd, Leicester, UK

Matador is an imprint of Troubador Publishing Ltd

This is the second book in the Hollie and Figgs series.
It is dedicated to my beautiful daughter Holly and our adorable cat Tiggs. Holly drew the initial illustrations for the first book, which began as a family project to help build her confidence when she wasn't well.

Since then, I have been taking our story into schools to inspire young children. I had such a positive response to the first story that I decided to write a second one.

My aim is to inspire children to be creative and never lose sight of their dreams.

It's been an absolute pleasure to work with student illustrator Beth Hilliard on this book. I know she will be very successful.

I'd like to dedicate this book to the amazing, talented children I met on school visits.

To keep up to date with Hollie and Figgs' adventures, visit them at:

www.hollieandfiggs.co.uk
www.facebook.com/Hollieandfiggs
www.instagram.com/hollieandfiggs
www.twitter.com/annettesharman

I hope you love our story and characters as much as we do.

Chapter 1

Hollie was a very lucky girl. She had a cat called Figgs. But he wasn't just *any* cat – he was a magical cat! When Hollie was sad after moving house and starting a new school, Figgs took her on an amazing adventure to the faraway kingdom of Hippogoblin Land, where friendly little creatures called Hippogoblins lived. Since then, Hollie has been a lot happier and has made new friends at school.

When Hollie visited Hippogoblin Land, she met Princess Lulubud, who was sad and lonely because she had no friends. Hollie suggested the princess should have a party to help her make friends. Her father, the king, agreed. Then Hollie and Figgs received a royal invite to Princess Lulubud's special ball...

Hollie hasn't been able to think about anything else, so she decided to have her own tea party in the garden with Figgs, just like the one they were invited to in Hippogoblin Land.

After a while, she lay down and looked up at the clouds, picturing the dazzling colours of the rainbow-lit sky in the magical kingdom. She imagined the sweet fragrance in the air, and burst into rhyme:

"Figgs, you're very special, you're my magic talking cat.
You take me to lands on my rainbow mat.
To magical places far, far away,
Where little princesses like to play."

She sighed. "I can't wait for the princess's ball. I wonder what it'll be like."

Figgs rubbed his head briskly against her hand, looked at her with his sparkly green eyes, and purred loudly.

All of a sudden, Hollie heard a voice calling her from the garden next door. It was Tommy, Hollie's neighbour.

"Hollie, do you want to play footy?" he yelled.

Just then, a ball hurtled over the garden fence, nearly hitting Figgs. He jumped high into the air, screeched, and landed on all four paws with a thud.

"Oh, Tommy, you just missed Figgs! Please stop kicking your ball over the fence!"

Tommy was the same age as Hollie and went to the same school, but he was in a different class. He had striking blue eyes, scruffy fair hair, and wore baggy shorts. He was always playing football. Hollie often heard his mum calling for him to do his homework.

Hollie has played football with him a few times, but preferred to play with Figgs.

Tommy told her that he doesn't like cats. A cat scared him when he was younger, and he has never got over it.

"If only Tommy knew that Figgs isn't like other cats, he'd be sure to like him," Hollie thought mischievously.

"Hollie, your tea's ready," her mum called from the kitchen.

"I can't play today, Tommy," said Hollie. "I have to go – my mum's calling me."

She tossed the ball back over the fence. Soon she could hear Tommy kicking the ball against the wall.

Chapter 2

After tea, Hollie sat down to do some homework before bedtime. But she couldn't concentrate. All she could think about was Princess Lulubud's ball.

"What will I wear? And what will the ball be like?" she wondered, full of excitement.

She got ready for bed and eventually drifted off to sleep. It wasn't long before morning arrived and it was time to get ready for school. She glanced over at the miniature daisy chain that the princess gave her when she left Hippogoblin Land. Normally flowers fade and die, but not these – and they smelled just like strawberry laces! Hollie spotted something else, sitting on her bedside table by the daisy chain, glistening in the morning sunlight. It was a miniature silver tiara. Hollie was confused. "How did that get here?" she thought.

She looked at Figgs. He looked up at her with the cheekiest grin on his face.

Did he know something she didn't?

He jumped down from the bed and meowed loudly to get Hollie's attention. There in his bed was a tiny green bow tie.

Hollie beamed at Figgs. "Are these for the princess's ball? I can't wait!"

She got ready for school in a flash.

When she got home, Figgs was waiting for her at the front door, as he always did. She scooped him up in her arms and ran upstairs to see the tiny gifts again.

"How are we going to wear these, Figgs? They're far too small for us!" she said.

Figgs just looked at her and purred.

Hollie couldn't wait for the evening to pass. She was more excited than she had ever been in her entire life.

That evening, Tommy called again for Hollie to play with him, but she was far too preoccupied to do anything apart from prepare for Princess Lulubud's ball.

The evening dragged. Every minute felt as though it lasted an hour. Hollie kept looking at the clock, wondering when she and Figgs would be flying off to Hippogoblin Land on their magical rainbow rug.

She got out her favourite pink party dress. "This will be perfect for the ball," she thought.

Eventually, it was time for bed. Hollie put on her pink silk dress and waited patiently, but nothing happened.

"I don't understand," she thought. "It's the 14th of June, so why aren't we going to the ball?"

Soon, she felt very tired and couldn't keep her eyes open any longer. Then she drifted into a deep sleep. All of a sudden, Figgs nudged her and jumped down from the bed. He sat on the round rainbow rug – their magic carpet – and called out, "Come on, Hollie, it's time to go!"

She was so sleepy that she had almost forgotten that Figgs was magic – and could talk! Figgs looked up at her with his sparkly green eyes, wearing a knowing grin. He was dressed in the green bow tie, and looked very stylish.

Hollie leapt out of bed as fast as she could and sat next to Figgs. A glittering tiara lay next to him. It was just like the miniature one, but this one was big enough for her to wear.

She popped it on her head. Then, with a twitch of Figgs' pink nose, off they flew.

After a while, the magic carpet landed. They looked all around them.

"Is this Hippogoblin Land? It doesn't look like it..."

Chapter 3

They'd landed in a dark forest that reeked of rotten leaves. Green slime dripped from branches high above them, and a chill breeze blew around them. Hollie was scared.

"W-w-where are we, Figgs?" she stuttered.

"I'm not sure," Figgs replied, looking puzzled. "That's never happened before. It looks as though we've gone off course."

The dark green trees loomed over them menacingly. The atmosphere was silent apart from the odd squawk, which made Hollie jump.

They could barely see the sky through the dense, leafy canopy.

Figgs glanced around. "This looks like Loppy Wood. I've heard about it, but I've never been here."

All of a sudden the trees started to sway slowly and shake their long, spindly branches.

"We'll have to try again," said Figgs. They jumped onto the magic carpet, but nothing happened.

Then they heard a crackly voice calling their names from what sounded like a long way off. "Is that you, Hollie and Figgs?"

Then a little creature sprang out into the open just in front of them. He was orange, smaller than Figgs, with scruffy fair hair and bright blue eyes. His clothes were old and tatty.

Figgs recognised his voice right away. "Thomasin? Is that you?"

Figgs introduced Hollie to Thomasin. He was a Chippogoblin from Chippogoblin Land, which borders Hippogoblin Land. Chippogoblins are very friendly, helpful creatures.

"This is all very confusing," thought Hollie.

"What are you doing here?" asked Figgs.

"I am your guide," said Thomasin. "The king sent me to find you. A few days ago, a dark cloud came over Hippogoblin Land. The king cannot make the cloud leave, and he fears that the land will never be the same again. Without the rainbow, he has no magical powers! He's cancelled Princess Lulubud's ball, but guests are still arriving. They're ending up in all sorts of odd places... He hopes that you will be able to help." Thomasin yanked up his ill-fitting trousers, rubbed his bulbous orange nose and said, "Follow me!"

They stayed close to him. As they walked, the trees' long branches swooped behind them, ushering them along the path. With every step, the trees rustled and moaned.

Figgs was more determined than Hollie had ever seen him. He was eager to get to the king as soon as he could.

Hollie thought about how Princess Lulubud might be feeling now that the ball had been cancelled. It had been a way for her to find friends and make her happy again.

Finally, they reached the end of the forest. Thomasin whistled a tune. In a flash, an enormous blue furry creature with a long striped tail appeared from nowhere. It screeched to a halt, only just missing them.

"Come on – climb on to Smudgers. He will take us to the king," said Thomasin.

As soon as they were all on Smudgers' back, the creature sprang into the air at such a speed that Hollie could hardly get her breath.

They could see the silhouette of the palace in the distance. Everything around it looked dark and dreary. The flowers in Hippogoblin Land were usually happy, and threw sweets and treats into the air for people who were passing by, but today even the flowers looked miserable.

Hippogoblin Land needed Hollie and Figgs' help!

Chapter 4

When they caught sight of the king on the lawn outside the palace, Smudgers drifted down and landed gently beside him.

"Your Majesty," said Figgs. "We're here to serve you. What can we do to help?"

The king replied, "Someone has stolen the rainbow and a huge black cloud has taken its place. Without the rainbow, I have no magical powers. I need your help to find it!"

The princess had tears in her eyes. She was very upset that her ball had been cancelled. "I've missed you, Hollie," she said.

"I've missed you too," said Hollie, squeezing Princess Lulubud's hand.

"Hollie, you stay with Princess Lulubud. I will take Thomasin to search for the rainbow," said Figgs.

Figgs and Thomasin mounted Smudgers' back again and they shot off. Smudgers didn't waste any time. He swooped and looped, swerved and dived, searching all over Hippogoblin Land and the neighbouring lands for the rainbow. He searched Gingerkin Land, Minty Wood, the Forest of Gloom and even the seas of Mermin Land, but the rainbow was nowhere to be seen.

Then Figgs spotted a colourful light shining out of a cave high in the mountains.

Could it be the rainbow?

As they approached the cave, they could see a small figure sitting on a rock near the cave's entrance. He was holding his head in his hands – or were they paws? As they got nearer, they could hear a screechy voice, wailing:

"Oh woe, oh no, how sad am I?
I stole the rainbow from the sky.
And now my sister can't have her ball.
I should be happy, but I'm not at all."

Figgs remembered that Hippogoblins often burst into rhyme when they were unhappy.

I know – what a funny thing to do!

Then he recognised the figure as the king's son. "Prince Zulubud? What's the matter?" Figgs asked.

"I have done something terrible," Prince Zulubud said. "I used my father's magic to steal the rainbow from Hippogoblin Land. It's in this cave."

Figgs and Thomasin looked shocked. Why would he do such a thing?

"I was jealous that my sister Princess Lulubud was having a ball. I took the rainbow – and all the colour – out of Hippogoblin Land, so the ball would have to be cancelled. Now my father has no magic and everyone will hate me. I don't know what to do."

Figgs sighed. "The first thing we must do is get the rainbow back to Hippogoblin Land."

Smudgers grabbed hold of the rainbow and pulled as hard as he could, but it wouldn't budge. He tugged and twisted and pulled and prised, but he just wasn't strong enough to move it.

Prince Zulubud mumbled, "It's the Polygrogs. When they saw that I had hidden the rainbow in their cave, they stole it from me and now they want to keep it for themselves. They said it brightens up their cave."

"What are Polygrogs?" asked Figgs.

"They're tiny, fearless creatures that live deep in the caves. No one has ever seen one, but legend says that if anyone sees a Polygrog they will turn into a Polyfrog – a slave to the Polygrogs. Polygrogs are ten times stronger than Smudgers."

"So how can we get the rainbow back and save Hippogoblin Land from an eternity of darkness, misery and no magic?" asked Thomasin.

Figgs thought for a while – then he had a clever idea.

Chapter 5

"If we can't match the Polygrogs' strength, then we must outwit them," said Figgs. "Prince Zulubud, what do Polygrogs eat?"

"I have been told that they eat slimy cave bugs," replied the prince.

"Right. If we can find some, you can entice them out with the bugs, and when the Polygrogs are eating the bugs we can snatch the rainbow," said Figgs.

Prince Zulubud found several of the slimiest, juiciest cave bugs you have ever seen and called out, "Mr Polygrog, I have a special treat for you!"

They heard a snorting and a snarling from inside the cave. The noise grew closer and closer, and made them shiver. They knew they mustn't catch sight of the cave creatures – or they might turn into Polyfrogs.

Figgs shouted, "Close your eyes, and then throw the creepy-crawlies into the cave."

Prince Zulubud hurled the yucky bugs towards the cave entrance. There were loud gnashing and gnawing sounds. Then, with their eyes closed, Figgs and Smudgers reached out towards the cave and grabbed hold of the rainbow. It slipped out of the cave with ease. Prince Zulubud, Thomasin and Figgs quickly jumped on to Smudgers' back and he leapt into the air. They whooshed through the sky, pulling the rainbow behind them.

As they approached Hippogoblin Land, the rainbow seemed to know it was home. It took a deep breath, grew bigger and bigger and bigger and bigger, and then sprang high into the sky until it covered the whole of Hippogoblin Land.

When they landed, the king, the queen, Princess Lulubud and Hollie ran over to them.

"You did it, Figgs!" said Hollie. "You're my hero!"

"Thank you, my friends," said the king. "You have served us well."

Prince Zulubud told his father how he'd used his magic to steal the rainbow in order to stop his sister's ball going ahead. The king and queen were very angry, and Princess Lulubud couldn't believe that her brother had been so mean.

The king said to his son, "Prince Zulubud, I am very disappointed in you. I know how much you love your sweet treats, so as a punishment you will have no sweets for a whole month.

"You must also promise that you will never do anything like this again. If you are unhappy about anything, then you must tell us."

Prince Zulubud was very sorry. He apologised to his sister for spoiling her ball. He had learned a very important lesson – and now he wanted to help his sister have the ball of her dreams.

The king invited everyone into the palace for the princess's ball – and to celebrate the return of the rainbow. So that Hollie and Figgs could join in the fun, the king used his magic to shrink them so they were the same size as everyone else.

Everyone was so happy and relieved to see that things were back to normal, they soon forgot all about the prince being jealous and stealing the rainbow.

The king addressed his people. "Thank you for coming to my daughter's ball and for making her happy."

The rainbow was delighted to be home. Its colours shone even brighter. Laughter echoed all around the palace.

Hollie danced for what seemed like hours with Princess Lulubud and her new friends. Figgs sat with Thomasin and ate some yummy treats. Prince Zulubud was very quiet, but relieved that everyone was still talking to him after what he'd done. Then came the finale: a breathtaking spectacle of twinkling fireworks popped all over the kingdom.

The princess had made some new friends, and the rainbow was back in Hippogoblin Land. Hollie and Figgs' job was done.

Figgs turned to Hollie. "It's time for us to go."

They said goodbye to everyone. The princess hugged Hollie. "I will miss you, Hollie," she said and thanked Figgs for finding the rainbow so that she could have her ball.

The king said to Figgs, "You are our faithful friend. We will never forget what you have done for us today."

This made Figgs feel very proud and like a true superhero.

The king was so pleased with Thomasin that he gave him a very important job in the palace, and Smudgers was allowed to stay in the palace courtyard to guard the royal family. He loved it, as it made him feel very special.

"Where's the magic carpet, Figgs?" asked Hollie.

"It's here, my dear," said the king. He swished his wand briskly and the magic carpet appeared before them.

With a twitch of Figgs' cute pink nose, off they flew. They soon found themselves back in Hollie's bedroom.

Then Hollie heard her mum calling her. "Are you ready for school yet?"

Hollie looked at Figgs. He meowed loudly and rubbed his head against her cheek.

"Wow – what an adventure we've had," she whispered in his ear. She looked over at her bedside table. On it sat the miniature tiara and tiny green bow tie. She grinned at Figgs, picked him up, and held him close to her.

After school that day, Hollie was playing in her garden when she heard someone calling her name. It was Tommy.

"Do you want to play footy?" he yelled.

He threw the ball over the fence. Before she could throw it back, he appeared at Hollie's garden gate. As he approached, Hollie noticed his blue eyes, scruffy fair hair and baggy shorts. She had to look twice. Who did he remind her of? Ah, yes – he looked just like someone she had met in Hippogoblin Land!

Lightning Source UK Ltd.
Milton Keynes UK
UKRC02n2009201117
313067UK00003B/69